MUMMY'S MAGICAL HANDBAG

Paulette Bogan

BLOOMSBURY
CHILDREN'S
BOOKS

First published in Great Britain in 2004 by Bloomsbury Publishing Plc
38 Soho Square, London W1D 3HB

Copyright © 2004 by Paulette Bogan
The moral right of the author/illustrator has been asserted

A CIP catalogue record of this book is available from the British Library

Designed by Marikka Tamura
Type set in Malloy
Illustrated in ink and watercolours

ISBN 0 7475 7064 7

Printed in Dubai

1 3 5 7 9 10 8 6 4 2

All papers used by Bloomsbury Publishing are natural, recyclable products made from
wood grown in well-managed forests. The manufacturing processes conform
to the environmental regulations of the country of origin.

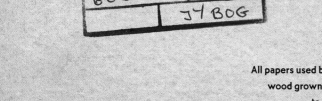

Love and thanks to Sophia, for all her help
And for our cool cousins,
Cassandra, Austin and Mackenzie

Cousin David never believed anything.
"My mummy has EVERYTHING in her handbag," said Rachael.
"She does not," said David.

"Everything," said Rachael.
"And the handbag is magic, too!"
"It is not!" said David.

"Children, are we going to argue, or are we going to the park?"
asked Mummy. She patted her handbag. "Now come along."

Rachael scratched her knee on a branch.

"OUCH!" she cried. "Mummy, I hurt my knee."

"Would a kiss make it better?" asked Mummy.

"And a plaster," said Rachael.

David rolled his eyes as Mummy pulled out a plaster.
"Everyone has plasters," said David. "That's not magic."

It was windy by the lake.
"Brrr," shivered Rachael.
"Mummy, I'm cold."

Mummy dug in her handbag. "Here, honey, try this," she said.

"That was just luck," said David.

"Thank you, Mummy," Rachael said.

"You're welcome," said Mummy.

"Mummy, did you bring anything to eat?"
asked Rachael. "We're getting hungry."
"Oh dear, is it lunchtime?" said Mummy,
and she opened her handbag.
"No way," grumbled David.

Mummy pulled out a perfect picnic lunch.

"Here we go!" Mummy said.
Rachael said, "See, it IS magic."

"Mummy, why do you have so many things in your bag?"
asked Rachael.
"Well," Mummy said, thinking carefully. "You never know
what you might need," and she smiled a mysterious smile.
David was not smiling.

All of a sudden it started to rain.

"Oh dear," said Mummy.
Soon umbrellas, wellington boots, and raincoats
were flying from her handbag.

David was dry, but he was not happy. There was something fishy about this handbag. He was going to have a look for himself.

"Let's see who can collect the most raindrops!"
said Rachael. "Mummy, do you have a bucket?"
"Just a minute, honey," said Mummy. "Let me look."

Mummy frowned as she rummaged through her handbag.
"This bag needs a good cleaning," she said, pulling out
one thing after another.
Rachael looked worried. David looked in the handbag.

"A-ha!" said Mummy. And she pulled out a
fly swatter. "No, that's not it."
Still no bucket.
Now Rachael was really getting worried.
Mummy always had everything in her handbag.

"Where is David?" asked Rachael.
Suddenly they heard a whimper.

"That pup's in trouble!" said Mummy.
"Watch my bag, Rachael, here I go!"
Mummy pulled out her Rescue Kit.

Mummy lassoed a log and stepped out on to the rope.

"Go, Mummy, go!" Rachael called. "Be careful!"

"Aarrooo!" howled David.

"Don't worry, David. My mummy's coming!" yelled Rachael.

Mummy and David tiptoed back to shore.
"Yay, Mummy!" said Rachael.

"This has been quite a day," said Mummy.

"At least it stopped raining," said David.

"Mummy," said Rachael, "I know what you need, and it's not in your bag."

Rachael gave Mummy a big hug and a kiss. So did David!

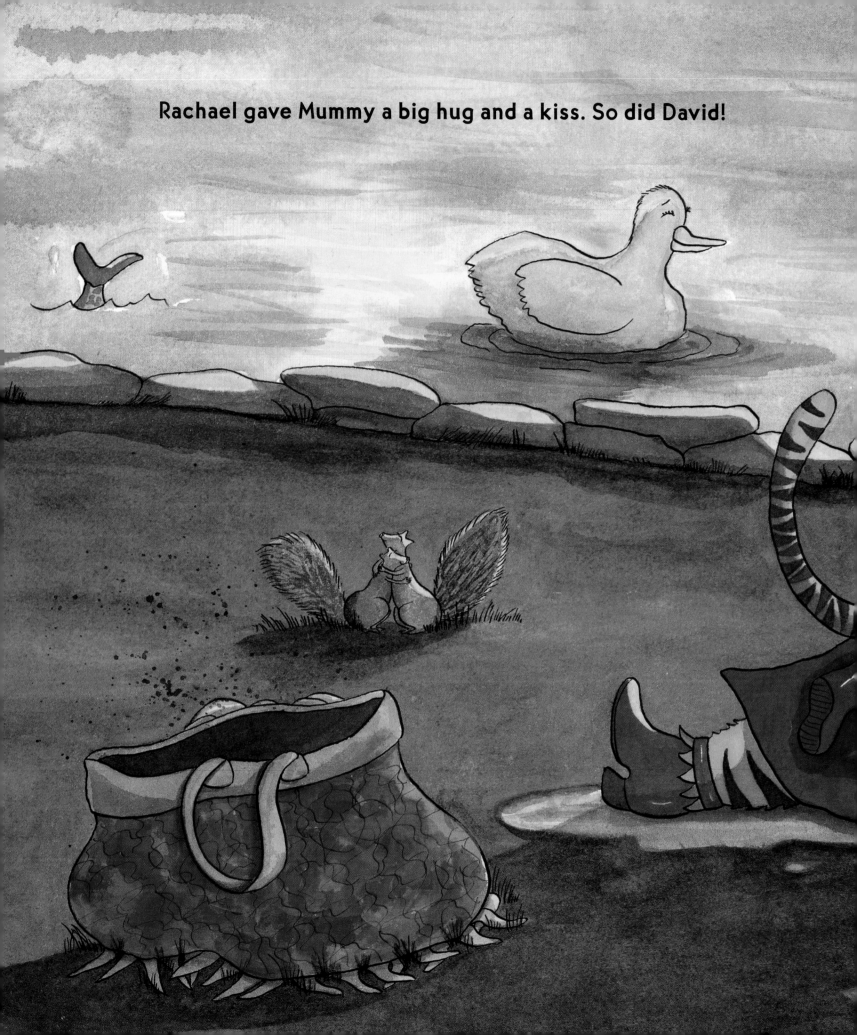

"Thank you, sweeties," said Mummy.

"That's just what I needed. Does anyone have a hankie?"